A GOLDEN BOOK • NEW YORK

Copyright © 2009 Disney Enterprises, Inc. Walt Disney's *Cinderella* copyright © 1998, 2005 Disney Enterprises, Inc. Walt Disney's *Snow White and the Seven Dwarfs* copyright © 1999, 2003 Disney Enterprises, Inc. Walt Disney's *Sleeping Beauty* copyright © 1997, 2004 Disney Enterprises, Inc. All rights reserved. Published in the United States by Golden Books, an imprint of Random House Children's Books, a division of Random House, Inc., 1745 Broadway, New York, NY 10019, and in Canada by Random House of Canada Limited, Toronto, in conjunction with Disney Enterprises, Inc. The stories contained in this work were originally published separately by Golden Books as follows: Walt Disney's *Cinderella,* illustrated by Ron Dias and Bill Lorencz, was originally published in 1998. Walt Disney's *Snow White and the Seven Dwarfs,* cover illustrated by Don Williams, was originally published in 1999. Walt Disney's *Sleeping Beauty,* adapted by Michael Teitelbaum and illustrated by Sue DiCicco, was originally published in 1997. Golden Books, A Golden Book, A Little Golden Book, the G colophon, and the distinctive gold spine are registered trademarks of Random House, Inc.
www.randomhouse.com/kids
Library of Congress Control Number: 2008928536
ISBN: 978-0-7364-2656-5
MANUFACTURED IN SINGAPORE
10 9 8 7 6 5 4 3 2 1

Once upon a time, in a faraway kingdom, there lived a widowed gentleman and his lovely daughter, Ella.

Ella was a beautiful girl. She had golden hair, and her eyes were as blue as forget-me-nots.

The gentleman was a kind and devoted father, and he gave Ella everything her heart desired. But he felt she needed a mother. So he married again, choosing for his wife a woman who had two daughters. Their names were Anastasia and Drizella.

The gentleman soon died. Then the Stepmother's true nature was revealed. She was only interested in her mean, selfish daughters.

The Stepmother gave Ella a little room in the attic, old rags to wear, and all the housework to do. Soon everyone called her Cinderella, because when she cleaned the fireplaces, she was covered with cinders.

But Cinderella had many friends. The old horse and
Bruno the dog loved her. The mice loved her, too. She
protected them from her Stepmother's nasty cat, Lucifer.
Two of her favorite mice were Gus and Jaq.

Cinderella was kind to everyone—even to Lucifer. But
Lucifer took advantage of her kindness.

Lucifer liked to get Cinderella in trouble. One morning, he chased Gus onto Anastasia's breakfast tray. She screamed and blamed Cinderella.

"Come here," the Stepmother said to Cinderella. "The windows—wash them! Then scrub the terrace, sweep the halls, and, of course, there's the laundry."

In another part of the kingdom, the King was worrying about his son. "It's high time he married and settled down!" he told the Grand Duke.

"But sire," said the Grand Duke, "we must be patient."

"No buts about it!" shouted the King. "We'll have a ball tonight. It will be very romantic. Send out the invitations!"

When the invitation arrived, Cinderella's Stepmother announced, "There's a ball! In honor of the Prince . . . every eligible maiden is to attend."

"That means I can go, too!" Cinderella said.

"Well, I see no reason why you can't," the Stepmother replied with a sly smile. "If you get your work done, and if you can find something suitable to wear."

Cinderella had hoped to fix her old party dress, but
Anastasia and Drizella wanted her to help them instead.

The Stepmother kept her busy, too.

Cinderella worked hard all day long. When she finally
returned to her little attic room, it was almost time to leave
for the ball. And her dress wasn't ready!

But the loyal mice had managed to find ribbons, sashes, ruffles, and bows. The mice had sewn them to her party dress, and it looked beautiful.

The stepsisters shrieked when they saw Cinderella. "They're my ribbons!" "That's my sash!" They tore her dress to shreds.

"Come along now, girls," said the Stepmother. And they left Cinderella behind.

Cinderella ran into the garden. She wept and wept.
Suddenly, a hush fell over the garden, and a cloud of lights began to twinkle and glow around Cinderella's head.

"Come now, dry those tears," said a gentle voice. Then a small woman appeared in the cloud. "You can't go to the ball looking like that. What in the world did I do with that magic wand?"

"Magic wand?" gasped Cinderella. "Then you must be . . ."

"Your Fairy Godmother," the woman replied, pulling her magic wand out of thin air. "The first thing you need is a . . . pumpkin."

A cloud of sparkles floated across the garden. A pumpkin rose up and swelled into an elegant coach. The mice turned into horses, the old horse became a coachman, and Bruno became a footman.

"Well, hop in, my dear," said the woman.

"But my dress . . . ," said Cinderella.

The Fairy Godmother looked at it. "Good heavens!" With a wave of her wand, she turned the rags into an exquisite gown. On Cinderella's feet were tiny glass slippers.

"You'll have only till midnight," the Fairy Godmother said. "At the stroke of twelve, the spell will be broken, and everything will be as it was before."

Cinderella promised to leave the ball on time. Then, under a shower of magic sparkles, she stepped into her coach and was swept away to the palace.

When Cinderella arrived at the ball, the Prince was yawning with boredom. Then he caught sight of her.

Ignoring everyone else, the Prince walked over to Cinderella. He kissed her hand and asked her to dance. They swirled off across the ballroom.

The Prince didn't leave Cinderella's side all night. They danced every dance together. As the lights dimmed and sweet music floated out into the summer night, Cinderella heard the clock begin to chime.

"Oh, goodness!" she gasped. "It's midnight. I must . . . Goodbye!"

"Wait! Come back!" called the Prince. "I don't even know your name!"

Cinderella hurried down the palace steps. In her haste, she lost one of the glass slippers, but she had no time to pick it up. She leaped into the waiting coach.

As soon as the coach went through the gates, the magic spell was broken. Cinderella found herself standing by the side of the road, dressed in her old rags. On one foot, she still wore a glass slipper.

Her coachman was an old horse again, and her footman was Bruno the dog. Her coach was a hollow pumpkin, and her horses were four of her mouse friends. They looked sadly at Cinderella.

They all hurried home. They had to be back before the others returned from the ball.

The next day, the Stepmother told the girls that the Grand Duke was coming to see them. "He's been hunting all night for that girl—the one who lost her slipper. That girl shall be the Prince's bride."

Cinderella smiled and hummed a waltz that had been played at the ball. The Stepmother became suspicious. She locked Cinderella in her room.

Gus and Jaq had a plan to help Cinderella. While Anastasia and Drizella tried to squeeze their big feet into the little glass slipper, the two mice sneaked into the Stepmother's pocket. They got hold of the key, tugged it upstairs, and unlocked the door. Cinderella rushed downstairs to try on the glass slipper.

"May I try it on?" Cinderella asked.

The wicked Stepmother fumed. She tripped the footman who was holding the glass slipper. It fell to the floor and broke into a thousand pieces.

"But you see," Cinderella said, reaching into her pocket, "I have the other slipper."

She put it on, and it fit perfectly!

From that moment on, everything was a dream come true. Cinderella went off to the palace with the happy Grand Duke. The Prince was overjoyed to see her, and so was the King.

Cinderella and the Prince were soon married.

In her happiness, Cinderella didn't forget about her animal friends. They all moved into the castle with her.

Everyone in the kingdom was delighted with the Prince's new bride. And Cinderella and the Prince lived happily ever after!

Snow White
and the SEVEN DWARFS

Long ago, in a faraway kingdom, there lived a lovely young princess named Snow White.

Her stepmother, the Queen, was cruel and vain. She hated anyone whose beauty rivaled her own—and she watched her stepdaughter with angry, jealous eyes.

The Queen had magic powers and owned a
wondrous mirror that spoke. Every day she stood
before it and asked:

"Magic Mirror on the wall,
Who is the fairest one of all?"
And every day the mirror answered:
"You are the fairest one of all, O Queen,
The fairest our eyes have ever seen."

As time passed, Snow White grew more and more beautiful—and the Queen grew more and more envious. So she forced the princess to dress in rags and work from dawn to dusk.

Despite all the hard work, Snow White stayed
sweet, gentle, and cheerful.

Day after day she washed and swept and
scrubbed. And day after day she dreamed of a
handsome prince who would come and carry her
off to his castle.

One day when the Queen spoke to her mirror, it replied with the news she had been dreading. There was now someone even more beautiful than the Queen. And that person was Snow White!

The Queen sent for her huntsman.

"Take Snow White deep into the forest," she said, "and there, my faithful huntsman, you will kill her."

The man begged the Queen to have mercy, but she would not be persuaded. "Silence!" she warned. "You know the penalty if you fail!"

The next day Snow White, never suspecting that she was in danger, went off with the Huntsman.

When they were deep in the woods, the Huntsman drew his knife. Then, suddenly, he fell to his knees.

"I can't do it," he sobbed. "Forgive me." He told her it was the Queen who had ordered this wicked deed.

"The Queen?" gasped Snow White.

"She's jealous of you," said the Huntsman. "She'll stop at nothing. Quick—run away and don't come back. I'll lie to the Queen. Now, go! Run! Hide!"

Frightened, Snow White fled through the woods. Branches tore at her clothes. Sharp twigs scratched her arms and legs. Strange eyes stared from the shadows. Danger lurked everywhere. Snow White ran on and on.

At last Snow White fell wearily to the ground and began to weep. The gentle animals of the forest gathered around and tried to comfort her. Chirping and chattering, they led her to a tiny cottage.

"Oh," said Snow White, "it's adorable! Just like a doll's house."

But inside, the little tables and chairs were covered with dust, and the sink was filled with dirty dishes.

"My!" said Snow White. "Perhaps the children who live here are orphans and need someone to take care of them. Maybe they'll let me stay and keep house for them."

The animals all helped, and soon the place was neat and tidy.

Meanwhile, the Seven Dwarfs, who lived in
the cottage, were heading home from the mine,
where they worked.

The Dwarfs were amazed to find their house so clean. They were even more amazed when they went upstairs and saw Snow White!

"It's a girl!" said Doc.

"She's beautiful," sighed Bashful.

"Aw!" said Grumpy. "She's going to be trouble! Mark my words!"

Snow White woke with a start and saw the Dwarfs gathered around her. "Why, you're not children," she said. "You're little men!"

"I read your names on the beds," she continued. "Let me guess who you are. You're Doc. And you're Bashful. You're Sleepy. You're Sneezy. And you're Happy and Dopey. And you must be Grumpy!"

When Snow White told the Dwarfs about the Queen's plan to kill her, they decided that she should stay with them.

"We're askin' for trouble," huffed Grumpy.

"But we can't let her get caught by that kwicked ween— I mean, wicked queen!" said Doc. The others agreed.

That night after supper, they all sang and danced and made merry music. Bashful played the concertina. Happy tapped the drums. Sleepy tooted his horn. Grumpy played the organ. And Dopey wiggled his ears!

Snow White loved her new friends. And she felt safe at last.

Meanwhile, the Queen had learned from her mirror that Snow White was still alive.

With a magic spell, she turned herself into an old peddler woman. She filled a basket with apples, putting a poisoned apple on top. "One bite," she cackled, "and Snow White will sleep forever. Then I'll be the fairest in the land!"

The next morning before they left for the mine, the Dwarfs warned Snow White to be on her guard.

"Don't let nobody or nothin' in the house," said Grumpy.

"Oh, Grumpy," said Snow White, "you *do* care! I'll be careful, I promise." She kissed him and the others good-bye, and the Dwarfs went cheerfully off to work.

A few minutes later, the Queen came to
the kitchen window.

"Making pies, dearie?" she asked. "It's apple pies
the men love. Here, taste one of these." She held
the poisoned apple out to Snow White.

Snow White remembered the Dwarfs' warning.
But the woman looked harmless, and the apple
looked delicious.

Snow White bit the apple. Then, with a sigh,
she fell to the floor.

Told by the birds and animals that something was wrong, the Dwarfs raced back to the cottage. They saw the Queen sneaking off, and they ran after her.

As storm clouds gathered and rain began to fall, the Dwarfs chased the Queen to the top of a high, rocky mountain.

Crack! There was a flash of lightning, and the evil queen fell to her doom below.

But it was too late for Snow White. She was so beautiful, even in death, that the Dwarfs could not bear to part with her. They built her a coffin of glass and gold, and day and night they kept watch over their beloved princess.

One day a handsome prince came riding
through the forest. As soon as he saw Snow White,
he fell in love with her. Kneeling by her coffin, he
kissed her.

Snow White sat up, blinked, and smiled. The
Prince's kiss had broken the evil spell!

As the Dwarfs danced with joy, the Prince
carried Snow White off to his castle, where they
lived happily ever after.

*L*ong ago, in a faraway land, King Stefan's fair queen
gave birth to a daughter. They named her Aurora.

To honor the baby princess, the king held a great
feast. Nobles and peasants, knights and their ladies—
everyone flocked joyfully to the castle.

King Stefan welcomed his good friend King Hubert
to the feast. King Hubert had brought his young son,
Phillip, with him. The kings agreed that someday
Phillip and Aurora would be married.

Among the guests were three good fairies, Flora, Fauna, and Merryweather. Each wished to bless the infant with a gift.

Waving her wand, Flora chanted, "My gift shall be the gift of Beauty."

"And mine," said Fauna, "shall be the gift of Song."

Merryweather was next. But before she could speak, the castle doors flew open.

Lightning flashed. Thunder rumbled. A tiny flame appeared and grew quickly into the form of the evil fairy Maleficent. Her pet raven was perched on her shoulder.

Maleficent was furious, for she hadn't been invited to the feast.
"I, too, shall bestow a gift on the child," she said with a sneer.
"She shall indeed grow in grace and beauty. But before the sun
sets on her sixteenth birthday, she shall prick her finger on the
spindle of a spinning wheel . . . and die!"

With a cruel laugh, Maleficent vanished. Everyone in the room
was grief-stricken.

But Merryweather still had a gift to give, and she
tried to undo Maleficent's curse. She said to the baby:
    "If through this wicked witch's trick
    A spindle should your finger prick,
    Not in death, but just in sleep
    The fateful prophecy you'll keep,
    And from this slumber you shall wake
    When true love's kiss the spell shall break."

King Stefan ordered that every spinning wheel in the land be burned.

But he still feared the evil fairy's curse, so the good fairies hatched a plan. They would take Aurora to live with them deep in the woods, safe from Maleficent.

The king and queen agreed. They watched with
heavy hearts as the fairies hurried from the castle,
carrying the baby princess.

To guard their secret, the fairies disguised
themselves as peasant women and changed Aurora's
name to Briar Rose. The years passed quietly, and Briar
Rose grew into a beautiful young woman.

At last the princess reached her sixteenth birthday. Planning a surprise, the fairies sent her out to pick berries. Fauna baked a cake for her, while Flora and Merryweather sewed her a new gown.

In a mossy glen, Briar Rose danced and sang with her friends, the birds and animals. She told them of her beautiful dream about meeting a tall, handsome stranger and falling in love.

A handsome young man came riding by. When he heard Briar Rose singing, he jumped from his horse and hid in the bushes to watch her. Then he reached out to take her hand.

Briar Rose was startled. "I didn't mean to frighten you," the man said, "but I feel like we've met before."

Briar Rose was very happy. She and her admirer gazed into each other's eyes. The young man didn't know she was Princess Aurora. And she didn't know he was Prince Phillip, to whom she had been promised in marriage many years before.

Back at the cottage, the fairies gave Briar Rose her birthday surprises. Then Briar Rose told them that she had fallen in love.

"Impossible!" they cried. They told her the truth at last—she was a princess betrothed at birth to a prince. Now it was time for her to return home. So poor Aurora was led away, longing for her handsome stranger.

Maleficent's raven, perched on the chimney of the cottage, had heard everything. It flew off to warn Maleficent that the princess was finally returning.

Maleficent sped to the castle. There, using her evil powers, she lured Aurora to a high tower. In the tiny room, a spinning wheel suddenly appeared.

"Touch the spindle!" hissed Maleficent. "Touch it, I say!"

The three good fairies rushed to the rescue, but they
were too late. Aurora had touched the sharp spindle and
instantly fallen into a deep sleep. Maleficent's cruel curse
had come true. With a harsh laugh, the evil fairy vanished.

The fairies wept. "Poor King Stefan and the queen," said Fauna. "They'll be heartbroken when they find out," said Merryweather. "They're not going to," said Flora. "We'll put them all to sleep until the princess awakens." So the three fairies flew back and forth, casting a dreamlike spell over everyone in the castle.

Meanwhile, Maleficent had captured Phillip and chained him up in her dungeon.

But the good fairies had other plans for him. Using their magic, they broke the chains. They armed the prince with the Shield of Virtue and the Sword of Truth. Then they sent him racing to the castle to awaken the princess.

When the evil fairy saw Phillip escaping, she hurled heavy boulders at him. But the brave prince rode on.

When Phillip reached Aurora's castle, Maleficent caused a forest of thorns to grow all around it. Phillip hacked the thorns aside with his powerful sword.

In a rage, the evil fairy soared to the top of the highest
tower. There she changed into a monstrous dragon. "Now
you shall deal with me, O Prince!" she shrieked.

Maleficent breathed huge waves of flame. Phillip ducked
behind his strong shield.

Thunder cracked! Flames roared around him! The prince fought bravely. Guided by the good fairies, he flung his sword straight as an arrow. It buried itself deep in the dragon's evil heart, and the beast fell to its death. Maleficent was no more.

Phillip raced to the tower where his love lay sleeping. Gently he kissed her. Aurora's eyes slowly opened.

Now everyone was awake. The king and queen were overjoyed to see their daughter again, and wedding plans were soon made.

The good fairies were blissful, too. It had all ended the way it should—happily ever after.